A PETITION

FOR

UNIVERSAL SUFFRAGE.

To the Senate and House of Representatives:

The undersigned, Women of the United States, respectfully ask an amendment of the Constitution that shall prohibit the several States from disfranchising any of their citizens on the ground of sex.

In making our demand for Suffrage, we would call your attention to the fact that we represent fifteen million people—one half the entire population of the country—intelligent, virtuous, native-born American citizens; and yet stand outside the pale of political recognition.

The Constitution classes us as "free people," and counts us *whole* persons in the basis of representation; and yet are we governed without our consent, compelled to pay taxes without appeal, and punished for violations of law without choice of judge or juror.

The experience of all ages, the Declarations of the Fathers, the Statute Laws of our own day, and the fearful revolution through which we have just passed, all prove the uncertain tenure of life, liberty and property so long as the ballot—the only weapon of self-protection—is not in the hand of every citizen.

Therefore, as you are now amending the Constitution, and, in harmony with advancing civilization, placing new safeguards round the individual rights of four millions of emancipated slaves, we ask that you extend the right of Suffrage to Woman—the only remaining class of disfranchised citizens—and thus fulfil your Constitutional obligation "to Guarantee to every State in the Union a Republican form of Government."

As all partial application of Republican principles must ever breed a complicated legislation as well as a discontented people, we would pray your Honorable Body, in order to simplify the machinery of government and ensure domestic tranquillity, that you legislate hereafter for persons, citizens, tax-p... s or caste.

Voting Rights

For justice and equality your petitioners will ever pray.

NAMES.	RESIDENCE.
Cady Stanton,	New York
Susan B. Anthony	Rochester – N. Y.
ntoinette Brown Blackwell	New York
[illegible]	Newark N. Jersey

WE DEMAND
VOTING RIGHTS NOW!
WE MARCH FOR
JOBS FOR
WE MARCH FOR
WE MARCH FOR

Voting Rights

Kremena Spengler

Living in AMERICA

CREATIVE EDUCATION

CREATIVE PAPERBACKS

Published by Creative Education and Creative Paperbacks
P.O. Box 227, Mankato, Minnesota 56002
Creative Education and Creative Paperbacks are imprints
of The Creative Company
www.thecreativecompany.us

Book design by Graham Morgan (www.bluedes.com)
Art direction by Tom Morgan
Edited by Jill Kalz

Images by Getty (SDI Productions), Library of Congress (Peter Pettus), National Archives, National Archives and Records Administration, Shutterstock (Al Teich, Joseph Sohm, Rosamar, Sharkshock), Unsplash (Tom Barrett, Unseen Histories), Wikimedia Commons (Henry Bryan Hall, Jr., Michael Fleshman, Michael Vadon, Pete Souza, Sen. Jeff Merkley, Thomas Nast, Yoichi Okamoto)

Library of Congress Cataloging-in-Publication Data
Names: Spengler, Kremena, author.
Title: Voting rights / by Kremena Spengler.
Description: Mankato, Minnesota : Creative Education, Creative Paperbacks, [2025] | Series: Living in America | Includes webography. | Includes bibliographical references and index. | Audience: Ages 12–15 years | Audience: Grades 7–9 | Summary: "A social studies title for young adults that examines the history of suffrage and how and when voters received voting rights in the United States of America. Includes sidebars, real-person profiles, a glossary, a timeline, and further resources"— Provided by publisher.
Identifiers: LCCN 2023047161 (print) | LCCN 2023047162 (ebook) | ISBN 9781640269132 (library binding) | ISBN 9781682774632 (paperback) | ISBN 9798889890812 (ebook)
Subjects: LCSH: Suffrage—United States—History—Juvenile literature. | Political participation—United States—History—Juvenile literature. | Voting—United States—History—Juvenile literature. | United States.
Voting Rights Act of 1965. | Minorities—Suffrage—United States—History—Juvenile literature. | Voter turnout—Social aspects—United States—Juvenile literature.
Classification: LCC JK1846 .S64 2025 (print) | LCC JK1846 (ebook) | DDC 324.6/20973—dc23/eng/20231219
LC record available at https://lccn.loc.gov/2023047161
LC ebook record available at https://lccn.loc.gov/2023047162

Printed in China

They Turned Out to Vote in Wisconsin During a Health Crisis. Here's Why.
ARE HUMAN RIGHTS
WE ARE ALL RELATED
FOR THE SCHOOLS
UDENTS DESERVE
ELEVATOR
STAIRS

UNIVERSAL SUFFRAGE

CONVENTION

TUESDAY & WEDNESDAY

Nov. 20th, 21st, at 10 A. M., and 3 and 7.30 P. M.

AT TWEDDLE HALL.

ELIZABETH CADY STANTON,

FRED'K DOUGLASS

CONTENTS

Introduction

It was 1965. For months, efforts to register Black voters in Alabama had been blocked. Thousands of peaceful demonstrators had been arrested, jailed, and beaten. Voting rights activists decided to take their case directly to Governor George Wallace. They would march 54 miles (87 kilometers) from Selma to the state capital of Montgomery. Wallace ordered state troopers to do "whatever it takes" to prevent the march.

On Sunday, March 7, about 600 people left a downtown church and walked, undisturbed, through Selma, toward the Alabama River. As they neared the bridge, they saw trouble waiting on the other side. A wall of state troopers stretched across the road. Behind them were sheriff's deputies, some on horseback, and dozens of white spectators with Confederate flags. The marchers pressed on until they were about 50 feet (15 meters) from the troopers.

Moments later, the troopers advanced, wielding clubs and bullwhips. They knocked marchers to the ground and beat them. Clouds of tear gas billowed. The marchers' terrified screams mixed with the bystanders' cheers.

Television cameras captured the moment. ABC interrupted a movie about Nazi war crimes to air the Selma footage. Nearly 50 million Americans who had tuned in to see the movie could not miss the historical resemblance.

Outrage swept the country. Selma's "Bloody Sunday" was a turning point in the voting rights movement.

E. A. DRIN
Coc
SIGN O

George Washington (*right center*) presided over the signing of the U.S. Constitution.

CHAPTER 1:

Fighting for Rights

The struggle for voting rights in the United States has been long and sometimes violent. Many groups have had to fight to have their voices heard. They include people of color, women, low-income people, **immigrants**, people with disabilities, former prisoners, and teens.

After the American Revolution (1775–83), the nation moved from British rule to developing its own government. The U.S. Constitution, adopted in 1787, empowered states to oversee federal elections. It did not specify who could vote. That detail was left to the states. In most cases, the vote was restricted to white men who owned land.

In the 1800s, a growing number of men began to press for expansion of **suffrage**. They did not feel that land ownership should be a requirement for voting. Many states removed it, opening the door to complete white male suffrage. But gender and race still restricted the ability of many citizens to participate in the voting process.

After the Civil War (1861–65), a group called the Radical Republicans took control of **Congress**. They were mostly white Northerners who wanted to limit the power of Southern states. The 13th Amendment to the Constitution had freed people from slavery. The Radical Republicans saw an opportunity to both help their own cause and extend suffrage to formerly enslaved Black men. In 1870, Congress approved, or ratified, the 15th Amendment. It gave voting rights to men of all races.

During this time, known as Reconstruction, Black men not only voted but also won seats in Congress. Hiram Revels and Blanche Bruce became the first Black people elected to the Senate. They represented the state of Mississippi. The next Black senator, Edward Brooke of Massachusetts, was not elected until 1967—nearly a century later.

Reconstruction ended in 1877. White Southerners seized the moment. They rolled back voting rights through literacy tests, English language requirements, "grandfather clauses," and poll taxes. The grandfather clauses limited voting to men whose male ancestors had been allowed to vote before 1867. The poll taxes required voters to pay to register to vote. All of these barriers hurt not just Black men, but also immigrants and poor whites.

In the 1960s, civil rights leaders organized many peaceful protests to bring attention to voting rights. The South responded with violence. The murder of voting rights activists in Mississippi and the attack by white state troopers on marchers in Selma gained national attention. Public horror at the brutality helped turn the tide. In 1965, Congress passed the Voting Rights Act with strong support from both major political parties. President Lyndon B. Johnson signed it, as Dr. Martin Luther King, Jr., Rosa Parks, and other civil rights heroes stood at his side.

The Voting Rights Act of 1965 outlawed literacy tests and other obstacles to voting. The 24th Amendment, passed in 1964, had abolished poll taxes in federal elections. The Voting Rights Act

Although Black men could begin exercising their right to vote in 1867, many white men were still bitterly opposed.

ZOOM IN: SENECA FALLS CONVENTION

In 1840, two determined women, Lucretia Mott and Elizabeth Cady Stanton (*pictured*), met for the first time at an anti-slavery convention in London, England. They could not participate in it, however, because they were female. The snub inspired them to work together to win rights for women.

In 1848, back in New York, Mott and Stanton hosted the Seneca Falls Convention. It was the first women's rights convention in the United States. The convention published a Declaration of Sentiments that called for voting rights for women and other reforms. It was modeled after the Declaration of Independence, but it contained an important revision: "all men *and women* are created equal."

THE GEORGETOWN ELECTION—THE NEGRO AT THE BALLOT-BOX.—[See page 162.]

directed the federal government to challenge poll taxes in state and local elections as well. Importantly, the law required states with a history of race-based **voter suppression** to gain federal pre-approval of any changes to their election rules.

Unlike Black men, who were given the right to vote by the Constitution but denied the vote by individual states, women found no help in the Constitution. The 14th and 15th Amendments defined citizens and voters as "male." Several generations of women's suffrage supporters lectured, wrote articles and letters, marched, and peacefully refused to comply with laws to change the Constitution.

Strategies for achieving their goal varied. Some leaders, such as Elizabeth Cady Stanton and Susan B. Anthony, argued that the 15th Amendment should be dropped in favor of a universal suffrage amendment. Others, including Lucy Stone and Julia Ward Howe, pursued a strategy of passing suffrage acts in each state. By 1912, nine states had adopted woman suffrage laws. Some suffragists used more aggressive tactics. They picketed, held silent vigils, and went on hunger strikes. Often supporters met with fierce resistance. Opponents heckled, jailed, and sometimes physically abused them.

By 1919, the women's suffrage movement had finally gained enough support. Congress, grateful for women's help during World War I (1914–18), passed the 19th Amendment. It was ratified in 1920. It stated that the right to vote should not be denied based on gender.

Yet, it did not give that right to *all* women. Black and other minority women remained unable to vote well into the 20th century.

The Indian Citizen Act of 1924 became the basis for giving American Indians the right to vote. While it allowed them to vote, it didn't enforce the right. Forty more years would pass until all U.S. states granted full suffrage to American Indians.

By the mid-1960s, all U.S. citizens over the age of 21 could vote—in theory. In 1971, the voting age was lowered to 18, thanks to the rise of student activism and the Vietnam War (1955–75). The idea was that if a person was old enough to go to war, they should be allowed to vote.

In the 1970s and 1980s, Congress took steps to make voting easier for other groups. In 1975, it added provisions to the Voting Rights Act of 1965 to protect language minorities. These amendments required places with high numbers of voters who spoke little or no English to provide voting materials in other languages. In 1984, Congress required states to improve access for elderly people and people with disabilities. In 1986 (and again in 2009), Congress passed laws that made voting easier for military personnel and their families stationed overseas.

In 1993, in response to record low interest in registering to vote, Congress passed the National Voter Registration Act. Known as "motor voter," this law required states to allow citizens to register to vote when they renewed their driver's licenses. The law also had states offer registration by mail and at offices offering public assistance. Within a year, more than 30 million people had registered, or updated their registration, because of the law.

ZOOM IN: FREEDOM SUMMER

In the summer of 1964, several civil rights organizations organized a voting rights movement in Mississippi called the Freedom Summer Project. One thousand out-of-state volunteers and thousands of Black Mississippians registered Black voters and raised awareness of voting rights. They organized meetings, protests, freedom libraries, and other events. Reports say 1,062 people were arrested, 80 Freedom Summer workers were beaten, 37 churches were bombed or burned, and 30 Black homes or businesses were bombed or burned. Because of their involvement in this movement, four civil rights workers and at least three Black Mississippians were killed.

Civil rights leader Martin Luther King, Jr. (*third from right*) watches U.S. president Lyndon B. Johnson sign the Voting Rights Act of 1965.

The close presidential election in 2000 led to a recount of the votes in Florida. The recount brought to light many problems: faulty voting equipment, bad ballot design, and inconsistent rules. It prompted Congress to pass the Help America Vote Act of 2002. This law required states to replace old equipment. It also required them to create statewide voter lists and to not turn away voters if their names were not on the lists.

In 2013, the Supreme Court struck down a key provision from the Voting Rights Act of 1965. States with a history of voter suppression would no longer have to pre-clear any voting policy changes with the federal government. This decision angered many activists. They said it would lead to new efforts to suppress "undesirable" voters.

CHAPTER 2:

How the System Works

U.S. president Barack Obama attends a campaign rally shortly before his reelection in 2012.

Today, thanks to the efforts of many generations of Americans, every U.S. citizen age 18 and older can vote in federal, state, and local elections. But how do Americans vote? Why is voting important? Can a single vote make a difference? To answer these questions, it is important to understand how the system works.

Federal elections occur every two years. Most people vote on Election Day. It is always the first Tuesday after the first Monday in November. Depending on where a person lives, however, the voting period may be extended to include **absentee ballots**, mail-in ballots, and early voting.

Every member of the House of Representatives, and about one-third of the Senate, is up for re-election in any given election year. A presidential election is held every fourth year. Midterm elections, or midterms, take place halfway between presidential elections.

Canon

SA
OUR 2016
sylvania
EAT AGAIN

ZOOM IN: ELECTORAL TRUMPS POPULAR

In the 2016 election, more people voted for Hillary Clinton than Donald Trump overall in California, Texas, and Pennsylvania—but Trump won the U.S. presidency. In California, 8.8 million people voted for Clinton, and 4.5 million people voted for Trump. So, Clinton won that state's 55 electoral votes. In Pennsylvania, 2.9 million people voted for Clinton and 3 million for Trump. So, Trump won that state's 20 electoral votes. In Texas, 3.9 million voted for Clinton and 4.7 million for Trump, giving him 38 electoral votes. In these three states, 15.6 million people voted for Clinton and 12.2 million for Trump. But Clinton got 55 electoral votes to Trump's 58.

U.S. president-elect Donald Trump thanks supporters following the 2016 general election.

Congressional elections determine who represents each state in Congress. They also decide which political party will hold a majority in each chamber of Congress for the next two years. The number of representatives a state has in the House depends on its population. It is updated every 10 years. Each representative in the House serves a specific congressional district for a two-year term. There are currently 435 members of the House. Senators serve six-year terms. There are 100 U.S. senators, 2 from each state.

State and local elections can take place in any year, at any time. Voters in each state may elect the governors and lawmaking bodies, or legislatures, of that state. A city may elect its mayor. There may be elections for judges and other local officials.

Primary elections, or primaries, precede most federal and state elections. Primaries help the major political parties select who will represent them in the **general election**.

Not all voting decisions are about who should hold office. Some ballots ask voters' opinion on taxes, proposed rules, or whether to build a new school. These are called **ballot measures** or **ballot initiatives**. From 2010 to 2020, 164 statewide ballot measures appeared on ballots.

In most elections, candidates are elected directly by the people. This is called the "popular vote." But the president and vice president are not elected directly by citizens. Instead, they are chosen by **electors** through a process called the Electoral College. The process of using electors comes from the Constitution. It was a compromise between the popular vote and a vote in Congress. Each U.S. state gets as many electors as it has members in Congress, both House and Senate. Including the 3 electors from

Washington, D.C., there are currently 538 electors in all. Who is chosen to be an elector, how, and when varies by state.

After a voter casts a ballot for president, their vote goes to a statewide tally. In 48 states and Washington, D.C., the winner receives all the electoral votes of that state. Two states, Maine and Nebraska, split their electors between the candidates based on each candidate's share of the popular vote. The Constitution does not require electors to vote for the candidate chosen by their state's popular vote. But some states do. The rare elector who votes for someone else may be fined, disqualified, replaced, or taken to court by their state.

A presidential candidate needs the vote of at least 270 electors—or more than half—to win. In most cases, a projected winner is announced on election night in November. But the actual Electoral College vote takes place in mid-December when the electors meet in their states. If no candidate receives the majority of electoral votes, the vote goes to the House. This has happened twice. The first time was following the 1800 presidential election, when the House chose Thomas Jefferson. Following the 1824 presidential election, the House selected John Quincy Adams as president. It is possible to win the Electoral College but lose the popular vote. This happened in 2016, 2000, and three times in the 1800s.

People who think that one vote in millions cannot make much difference should consider some of the closest elections in U.S. history. In 2000, Al Gore narrowly lost the Electoral College vote to George W. Bush. The election came down to Florida, where Bush had won

Electoral College certificates are brought before Congress in ceremonial wooden boxes to be formally counted.

the popular vote by such a small margin that it triggered an automatic recount of votes. In the end, Bush won Florida by 0.009 percent of the votes cast in the state, or 537 votes. Had 600 more pro-Gore voters gone to the polls in Florida that November, Bush may never have been president, let alone a two-term president.

Donald Trump defeated Hillary Clinton in 2016 by securing a close Electoral College win. Although the election did not come down to a handful of votes in one state, Trump's votes in the Electoral College decided a tight race. Clinton had won the national popular vote by nearly three million votes. But the concentration of Trump voters in key districts in "**swing states**," such as Wisconsin, Pennsylvania, and Michigan, helped Trump secure enough electoral votes to win the presidency. In swing states, voters are almost evenly split between the two major political parties.

A single vote may not directly elect the president, but if a vote joins enough others, it matters when it comes to electoral results. There are also the local and state elections to consider. While presidential or other national elections usually get significant **voter turnout**, local elections don't. They are often decided by a much smaller group of voters. A Portland State University study found that fewer than 15 percent of eligible voters voted for mayors, council members, and other local offices. Low turnout means that important local issues are determined by a limited group of voters, making a single vote even more meaningful.

ZOOM IN: NEW JERSEY FLIP-FLOP

In the late 1700s, New Jersey gave women the right to vote—then took it away. The state's first constitution in 1776 gave suffrage to *all* residents, regardless of gender or race. Voters were simply required to be of age, hold property of a certain value, and have lived in the county for one year. Because married women couldn't own property, only single women were allowed to vote. Black people could vote if they met the residency and property requirements. In 1807, however, the state changed its mind and restricted voting rights to tax-paying, white, male citizens.

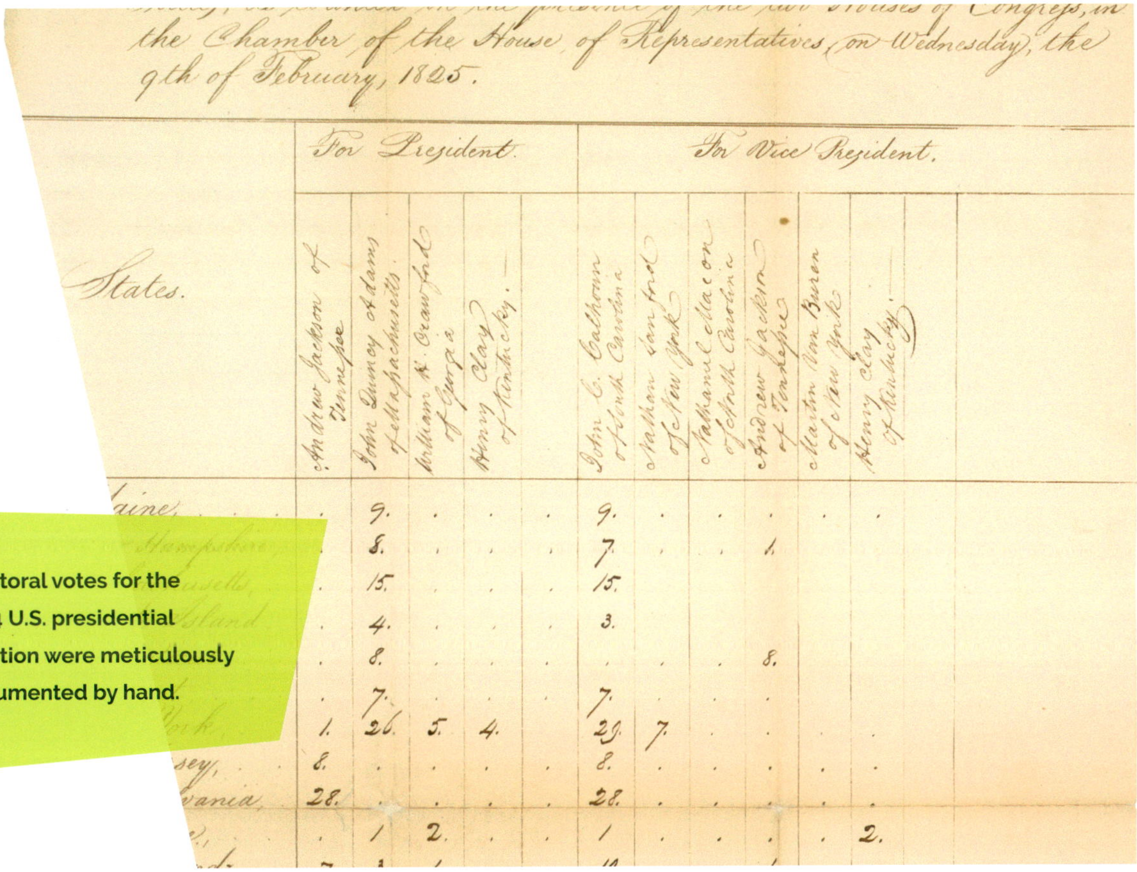

Electoral votes for the 1824 U.S. presidential election were meticulously documented by hand.

Some Americans believe that the U.S. electoral system does not accurately represent the will of the people. They think that the Electoral College is outdated, and that the president, too, should be elected directly. Over the past 200 years, more than 700 proposals have been introduced in Congress to reform or eliminate the Electoral College. There have been more proposals for constitutional amendments on changing the Electoral College than on any other subject. But other Americans support the system as designed. They say it helps prevent big states from dominating in national life. It protects the interests of smaller or less populous states and better reflects the diversity of the regions.

CHAPTER 3:

Voting Process

In most states, the voting process starts with registration. Voter registration is required in every state except North Dakota. Voters can register online, by mail, or in person. In-person registration can be completed at a Department of Motor Vehicles office, an armed forces recruitment center, or a public assistance office. If a voter changes their name, or moves to a new address or new state, they must update their registration.

A voter registration card confirms that a person is registered to vote. Voters do not necessarily need to bring this card to their **polling place**. However, they may need other identification. Some states require a photo ID, such as a driver's license, state ID, or passport. Other states accept a birth certificate or a Social Security card.

Even if a voter does not have the state-required ID, they may still be able to vote. Some states ask voters to sign a form affirming their identity. Others let them cast a **provisional ballot**.

In 2012, U.S. president Barack Obama (*left*) cast his general election vote at a Chicago, Illinois, community center.

ZOOM IN: NO REGISTRATION NEEDED

North Dakota is the only U.S. state without voter registration. This rural state maintains several small precincts to make sure election officials know their voters. Most precincts use a list of voters from previous elections. Voters simply show an ID and are checked off. Precincts without a list of previous voters use a blank poll book. As each voter's name and address is verified, the information is entered in the book. If a voter's eligibility is questioned, they may be asked to sign a form stating they can legally vote. If they sign, they must be allowed to vote.

States keep such ballots separate from other ballots while they verify the voter's eligibility. The voter may have to return to show their ID within a few days, or their provisional ballot will not count.

A voter's polling place is based on their home address. Voters need to vote at their assigned place. Their names will not be on the roster at any other location. Polling places are usually schools, community centers, and other public facilities. The site may change from one election to the next, so voters need to stay informed.

Voter guides and sample ballots include the candidates and the state or local issues that are up for a vote. Reviewing them before going to the polls can help people decide who and what to vote for. The voter guides offer details on each candidate's experience and goals. They also explain the ballot measures. Local newspapers often produce voter guides, as do other organizations. Sample ballots simply list the elections, candidate names, and measures that will be on the real ballot. Voters may bring their notes, a voter's guide,

Presidential candidates on general election ballots are grouped by political party.

OFFICIAL BALLOT, GENERAL ELECTION
PALM BEACH COUNTY, FLORIDA
NOVEMBER 7, 2000
(REPUBLICAN)
GEORGE W. BUSH - PRESIDENT
DICK CHENEY - VICE PRESIDENT
3
(DEMOCRATIC)
AL GORE - PRESIDENT
JOE LIEBERMAN - VICE PRESIDENT
5
(LIBERTARIAN)
HARRY BROWNE - PRESIDENT
ART OLIVIER - VICE PRESIDENT
7
(GREEN)
RALPH NADER - PRESIDENT
WINONA LaDUKE - VICE PRESIDENT
9
(SOCIALIST WORKERS)
JAMES HARRIS - PRESIDENT
MARGARET TROWE - VICE PRESIDENT
11
(NATURAL LAW)
JOHN HAGELIN - PRESIDENT
NAT GOLDHABER - VICE PRESIDENT
13
4
6
8
10
A
es will
electors.)

At national conventions, delegates vote for the presidential candidate they want to represent their party on the general election ballot.

Delegates gathered in the Chicago Coliseum for the 1912 Republican National Convention.

or a sample ballot into the voting booth, which frees them from having to memorize their choices.

Absentee voting allows voting before Election Day by mail or drop box. Although every state has absentee voting, deadlines vary, as do rules on who can take part. In most states, voters need to request an absentee ballot. Early voting allows voting in person before Election Day. In most states, people do not need an excuse to vote early.

A voter's political party affiliation is the party that they choose to associate with. Depending on their state, a voter may be asked for their party affiliation when they register to vote. Voters do not have to join a political party. They don't have to reveal it, either. Party affiliation does not limit a person to voting for just that party, especially in a general election. It is usually only important in some primary elections.

Some groups of people are not allowed to vote. Non-citizens, including permanent legal residents, cannot vote in federal, state, and most local elections. People with felony convictions or those serving time for some other types of crimes can't, either. Neither can people who are considered mentally incapacitated by the courts. Rules are different in each state.

CHAPTER 4:

Barriers to Voting

The population that turns out to vote often differs notably from the U.S. population at large. It is "whiter," "richer," and "older." That said, the gap between white and Black voting rates has narrowed since 2008 in both presidential elections and midterms.

White voter turnout rate is still almost 20 percent higher, however, than Asian or Latino voter turnout in both types of elections. People age 65 and older still vote at a rate almost 30 percent higher than 18- to 24-year-olds. The turnout rate among people earning between $100,000 and $150,000 per year remains 30 to 50 percent higher than the rate for those earning less than $20,000.

Voting rights activists claim that some state lawmakers put policies in place that make it harder for certain groups to vote. Officials sometimes justify these policies with the need to prevent voter fraud or increase election security. They say lack of funding is behind the policies and nothing more.

FUND CU
THE PEO
UNIVE
PSC-
VOTER
SUPPRESSION
PROTECT
VOTER
RIG
LISTEN TO
THE 99%
PROTECT
VOTER RIGHTS
HARRY T. & HARRIETTE
MOORE
UFT

ZOOM IN: NOT WORTH THE RISK

Some people claim that non-citizens (individuals who are nationals of countries other than the United States) unlawfully vote in U.S. elections. However, several studies and state-led investigations have shown that non-citizen voting in federal and state elections rarely happens. Doing so is illegal. If a foreign national intentionally registers or votes in one of those elections, they will face steep fines, prison, or being sent back to their home country. Very few non-citizens are willing to risk those consequences for one vote.

False claims of voter fraud have been used to justify strict voting requirements, such as a photo ID. Before 2006, no state required an ID to vote; today, 34 states do. A driver's license is the most common photo ID in the United States, so this requirement affects people who don't drive—namely, the young, the elderly, low-income people, or people with disabilities. Laws requiring a physical street address single out groups that are more likely to have P.O. Box addresses, such as American Indians living on reservations.

Other measures also disadvantage specific groups. For example, some local authorities are not translating materials or offering language assistance, as required by law. It is a barrier to voting for many people in the Asian American and Latino communities. A *USA Today* report found that election officials have closed thousands of polling places, largely in communities of color. For example, in Chicago's Cook County, which has the largest Black population in the country, election administrators closed or moved 95 polling places. With fewer polling places, voters' waiting times in mostly Black neighborhoods are 29 percent longer than in mostly white neighborhoods. Rather than wait, Black voters may choose not to vote.

ZOOM IN: BUILDING WALLS

In 2023, the trend was to increase accessibility for voters across the United States. Michigan, for example, eased restrictions on student IDs at polling places and expanded early voting. It also improved the process for tracking mail-in ballots. However, some states continued to pass restrictive laws. Arkansas and South Dakota, for example, got rid of ballot drop boxes. Lawmakers there claimed the boxes invited voter fraud. Opponents say that isn't true, that drop boxes make voting easier and allow more people to exercise their right to vote. South Dakota, for one, had no reported incidents of ballot box fraud in 2020 or 2022.

States and cities have long used early voting to reduce Election Day crunch. It opens up voting to people with work or other commitments. Faith groups have also used early voting in non-partisan get-out-the-vote efforts. But sometimes officials across the nation limit early voting or reduce voting hours. Doing so can make voting less convenient—or impossible. Low-income and working-class people often have less freedom to arrive late or leave early from work. They may not be able to take a break from their shifts in the middle of the day to vote. They can't afford to wait in long voting lines. Parents with inflexible childcare arrangements can also be affected.

A lack of funding is also a barrier to voting. Limited resources make it difficult for local governments to manage elections in a way that makes sure everyone's vote counts equally. This problem came to light in Florida during the 2000 presidential election. The Florida recount revealed issues ranging from flawed ballot designs to voting machines that overheated and failed.

Federal law allows voters whose eligibility is in question to use a provisional ballot. However, local governments set their own rules about how many provisional ballots to print. They also decide how to train poll workers on processing them. Some places do not print enough ballots. Other places have turned away eligible voters or thrown out their provisional ballots because of inadequate poll worker training. Poll workers need good training to follow the right policies: to properly check IDs, give language help, identify cases of voter intimidation, and offer provisional ballots. Yet, some poll workers are poorly equipped to do their job. They often lack the funding, or the commitment, to make voting welcoming and convenient.

CHAPTER 5:

Raising Turnout

A small number of countries, notably Australia, have mandatory "civic duty" voting. Some people have suggested that the United States do the same. Mandatory voting could involve steps such as moving Election Day to a weekend or making it a national holiday. However, not many scholars think these changes are likely to happen.

Regardless of what people think of mandatory voting, most agree that steps can be taken to make it easier to vote in the current system. There are reasonable ways to raise voter turnout rates. Proposals include more opportunities to register, more ways to cast a vote, and increasing funding for the election process.

According to historians, the requirement to register in advance of voting was meant to prevent immigrants arriving in the late 19th century and early 20th century from voting. Paired with poll

Prior to the 2020 U.S. election, casting a ballot in person was the most common method of voting.

ZOOM IN: MAIL-IN BALLOT FRAUD?

Some people believe everyone should vote in person only. They claim that drop boxes, voting by mail, and absentee voting are vehicles for mass voter fraud. But mail-in ballots have been used in the United States for more than 150 years. Voting rights advocates say it is more likely that someone will be struck by lightning than commit mail-in ballot fraud. Drop boxes are monitored by video surveillance, or with bipartisan teams of election workers, to make sure that votes are not stolen or tampered with. Bipartisan teams are usually present when mail-in ballots are handled, including when they are processed and counted.

taxes, it was also meant to discourage Black voters. In the days of paper and pencil, it may have been necessary to give officials enough time to prepare accurate voter lists. But today's technology and digital voting rolls have made this need outdated. Same-day registration encourages new voters. It also allows existing voters to update or correct errors in their registration.

Same-day registration was first adopted in the mid-1970s in Maine, Minnesota, and Wisconsin. Studies show that it has increased voter participation without major problems. The number of states that now offer same-day registration has grown. In 2020, 21 states and Washington, D.C., offered people the opportunity to use it. It made a difference. States with same-day registration had turnout rates 5 percent higher than states without it.

Twenty states and Washington, D.C., have also adopted policies that automatically register citizens to vote. People are given the opportunity to opt *out* of registering, rather than opt in. Oregon was the first state to do this, in 2016. In that year alone, more than 225,000 residents were automatically registered through Oregon's Department of Motor Vehicles.

Forty states and Washington, D.C., allow people to register to vote online. This cost-saving measure, first offered in Arizona in 2002, has eased voting registration for many people. The COVID-19 pandemic was a strong reason to start online registration, as options for in-person registration disappeared in 2020.

Twenty-three states also allow young people to pre-register before they are 18 years old. The individuals' names are then automatically placed on the rolls on their 18th birthday. Pre-registration enables high schools to educate students in civics and voting before students leave for college or join the workforce. Studies show that early registration makes it more likely that young people will become voters when they reach voting age. Related proposals call for letting 16- or 17-year-olds vote in local elections. Starting early would help them learn the process.

Along with expanded online registration, expanded early voting was a change made during the COVID-19 pandemic. Forty-three states and Washington, D.C., allow people to vote before Election Day. In the 2020 election, 25 percent of voters cast their votes early in person. A 2020 study on the impact of early voting in Ohio by the *American Economic Journal* found "substantial positive impacts of early voting on turnout." Widely available early voting also improves the experience for Election Day voters. It shortens lines and wait times.

The number of days that early voting is permitted varies greatly among states. For example, early voting in Florida must begin at least 10 days before an election, while Virginia passed a law in 2020 allowing 45 days of early voting. Supporters suggest that states offer at least 15 days of early voting.

During the 2020 election, many people voted by mail. While all states had increases in turnout compared to 2016, the states that had full or close-to-full voting by mail had a 9 percent increase in turnout. States that did not have it had a 5 percent increase. Many states mailed ballot applications or ballots to every voter. Although most states at first made this change only for the pandemic year, some states have made it permanent.

During the 2020 pandemic, states invested in making polling places safer. These efforts could be useful after COVID-19, too. During curbside voting, for example, poll workers took ballots or portable machines to voters' cars, removing the need to stand in line. Some places used mobile voting centers. The use of drop

To avoid contracting COVID-19 in crowded polling places on Election Day 2020, many people opted to vote early.

STACEY ABRAMS

Stacey Abrams is a prominent Black politician. She is known for her work to increase voting accessibility and turnout, especially for people of color.

In 2006, Abrams was elected to the Georgia House of Representatives. In 2010, she became the first Black person to be elected House minority leader. In 2013, she created a voter registration non-profit called The New Georgia Project. It helped complete 86,000 new voter applications, many of which came from voters of color.

Abrams rose to national fame when she ran for governor of Georgia in 2018. While she lost that race by about 55,000 votes, her candidacy was historic. When she won the Democratic primary in that race, she became the first Black woman to receive a major party's nomination for governor. During her campaign, she focused on bringing new voters to the polls.

Abrams continues to help with voter registration. She founded Fair Fight Action in 2018. Fair Fight is an organization that addresses the issue of voter suppression. Abrams is credited with being one of the major forces behind Democrats' wins in Georgia in the 2020 U.S. presidential and Senate races. She has started and inspired many organizations that work to register and turn out voters, particularly young voters and voters of color. For her work, Abrams has received numerous awards. In 2021, she was nominated for the Nobel Peace Prize.

Timeline

1700s

Voting is generally limited to white, male property holders.

1800s

Official voting barriers start to fall away.

1870

The 15th Amendment gives Black men the right to vote.

1920

The 19th Amendment gives women the right to vote.

1924

The Indian Citizen Act enables American Indians to vote.

1877–1960s

Southern states build barriers to voting, especially for people of color.

1964

The 24th Amendment bans poll taxes.

1965

The Voting Rights Act prohibits voter discrimination based on race, color, or membership in a language minority group.

1971

The 26th Amendment lowers the voting age from 21 to 18.

1975

The Voting Rights Act is expanded to protect language minorities.

1984

The Voting Accessibility for the Elderly and Handicapped Act requires polling places to be accessible to people with disabilities.

1986

The Uniformed and Overseas Citizens Absentee Voting Act allows members of the U.S. armed forces and U.S. voters abroad to register and vote by mail.

1993

The National Voter Registration Act creates new ways to register to vote.

2002

The Help America Vote Act authorizes federal funds for elections.

2009

The Military and Overseas Voting Empowerment Act improves access to voting for military voters and voters living outside the country.

2013

States with a history of discrimination no longer need to gain federal approval before changing their election rules.

2020

President Donald Trump claims widespread election fraud following his loss to Joe Biden, which is later proven false.

Glossary

absentee ballot—a vote cast by mail because a voter is absent from their usual polling place on Election Day

ballot measure (ballot initiative)—a law, issue, or question to be voted on that appears on a statewide or local ballot

Congress—the U.S. government's lawmaking body that is made up of the Senate and the House of Representatives

elector—a person who represents their state as part of the Electoral College process of electing the U.S. president

general election—a regular election of candidates for office, as opposed to a primary election

immigrant—a person who comes to live permanently in a foreign country; a foreign-born resident

polling place—the site where voters cast ballots in person

primary election—a preliminary election to choose a candidate who will represent a political party in a general election

provisional ballot—a preliminary ballot cast by a voter whose name is not on voting lists

suffrage—the right to vote

swing state—a state whose voters are almost evenly split between the two major political parties

voter suppression—efforts to keep people from casting ballots

voter turnout—the percentage of people who take part in an election

Selected Bibliography

Anderson, Carol. *One Person, No Vote: How Voter Suppression Is Destroying Our Democracy.* New York: Bloomsbury Publishing, 2018.

Berman, Ari. *Give Us the Ballot: The Modern Struggle for Voting Rights in America.* New York: Farrar, Straus and Giroux, 2015.

Dionne, E. J., Jr., and Miles Rapoport. *100% Democracy: The Case for Universal Voting.* New York; London: The New Press, 2022.

Fraga, Bernard L. *The Turnout Gap: Race, Ethnicity, and Political Inequality in a Diversifying America.* Cambridge, United Kingdom; New York: Cambridge University Press, 2018.

Litt, David. *Democracy in One Book or Less: How It Works, Why It Doesn't, and Why Fixing It Is Easier Than You Think.* New York: Ecco, 2020.

Smith, Erin Geiger. *Thank You for Voting: The Maddening, Enlightening, Inspiring Truth about Voting in America.* New York: Harper, 2020.

Waldman, Michael. *The Fight to Vote.* New York: Simon & Schuster, 2016.

Websites

Library of Congress: The Right to Vote
https://www.loc.gov/classroom materials/elections/right-to-vote

Explore the history of voting rights in the United States.

National Archives: African American Heritage
https://www.archives.gov/research/african-americans/vote

Discover facts about Black Americans and the vote.

National Women's History Museum
https://www.crusadeforthevote.org

Learn about the women's suffrage movement.

Index